The Spider's Journey

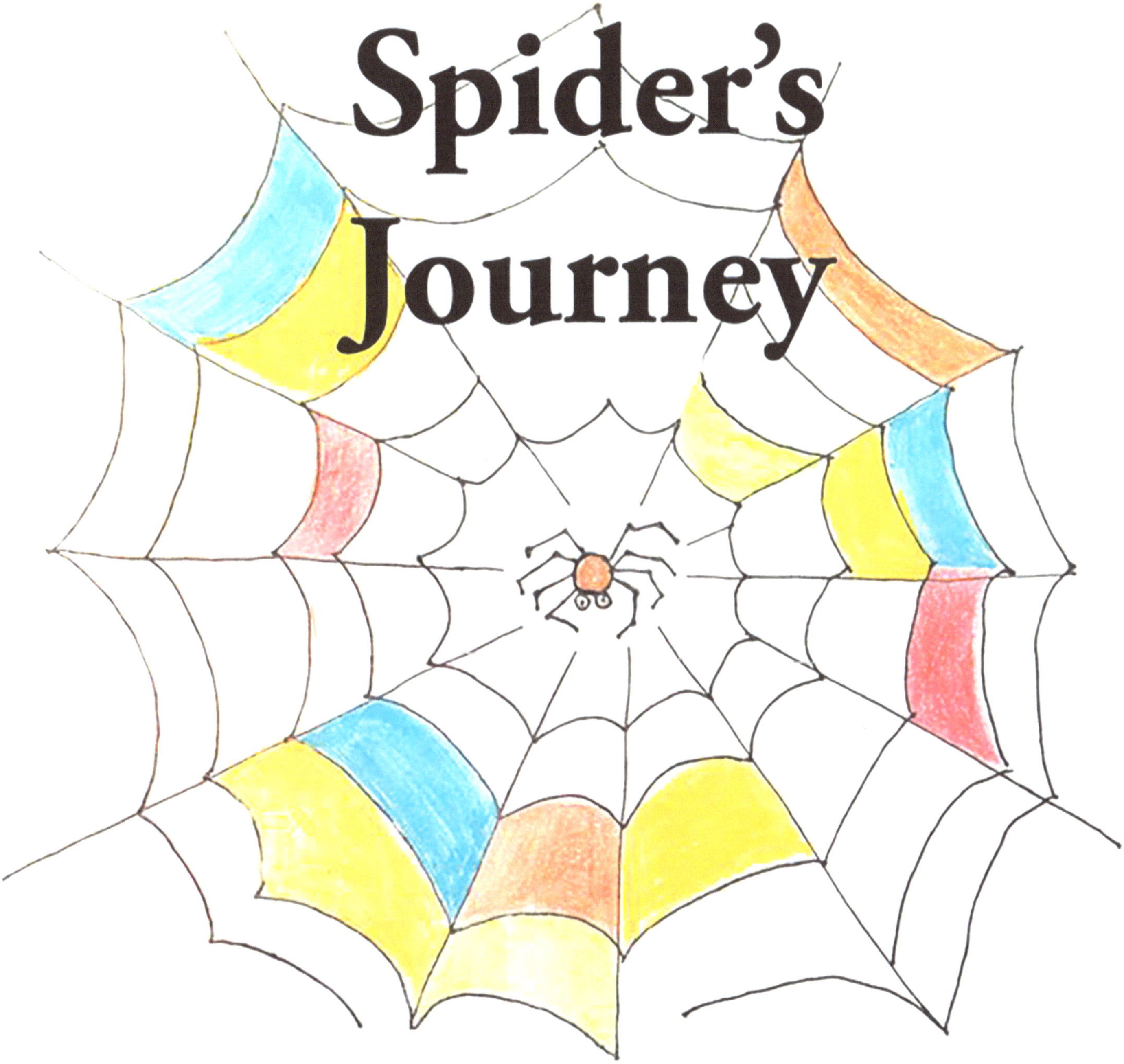

KATE GARDNER

Copyright © 2022 by Kate Gardner

ISBN: 978-1-990695-16-2 (Paperback)

           978-1-990695-17-9 (E-book)

All rights reserved. No part of this publication may be reproduced, distributed, or transmitted in any form or by any means, including photocopying, recording, or other electronic or mechanical methods, without the prior written permission of the publisher, except in the case brief quotations embodied in critical reviews and other noncommercial uses permitted by copyright law.

The views expressed in this book are solely those of the author and do not necessarily reflect the views of the publisher, and the publisher hereby disclaims any responsibility for them.

BookSide Press
877-741-8091
www.booksidepress.com
orders@booksidepress.com

The
Spider's
Journey

KATE GARDNER

To my mother, my father, my sisters, my brother, my husband, my son, his wife, my grandchildren Luke and Emily, and all my students who I know would have loved this book.

It was dusk and the glowing sun sparkled orange and gold over a quiet meadow. A spider was hiding in his web among the jagged branches of a blackberry patch. He was patiently waiting in his retreat waiting for a vibration that would announce his evening meal.

The sweet aroma of blackberries clung to the air, and a medley of a few brave crickets echoed through the field, bidding the sun farewell as it dropped from the sky.

The spider suddenly sensed something. His web began to violently shake, and he was thrown into the air.

He fell down, down, down for what seemed like forever and landed in a great hole. Before he was able to move, a huge blackberry hit him, then another, and another until he was completely trapped.

Soon the berries began to shake up and down, and he was bounced back and forth for another eternity.

    The spider was just about to give up all hope when everything became still.

He mustered up all his strength and crawled up the side of the "hole." When he reached the top, he quickly surveyed the area and crawled out.

Immediately, he saw a huge waterfall and inched a little closer to get a better view. Then a loud screeching sound and a large thud sent him running in the opposite direction.

He felt something hit him on one of his back legs, and he ran even faster. Luckily, he spied a crack and darted into it. It was very dark, but he felt safe there. Oh, how he wished he could be back in his web in the blackberry patch!

He heard a voice say, "Bob, hurry, come and kill this horrible spider! It's the ugliest one I've ever seen!"

Soon a man came near. He had very kind eyes. As he peered into the crack, he said, "He won't hurt you. See how pretty he is! Come on out spider!"

The woman stood far away with a rolled-up newspaper clutched in her hand, the one she had tried to kill him with. The spider backed as far as he could into the crack but could go no further.

"We shouldn't kill spiders," said the man with the kind eyes. "They are very useful creatures. They kill harmful insects and keep the woods healthy."

The man pushed a paper towel up to the crack and pulled the spider out. "See, he won't bite you if you don't handle or molest him."

The woman slowly edged nearer and by this time had dropped her newspaper. "He is very beautiful! Let's put him back outside in the blackberry patch!"

www.ingramcontent.com/pod-product-compliance
Lightning Source LLC
LaVergne TN
LVHW070454080526
838202LV00035B/2829